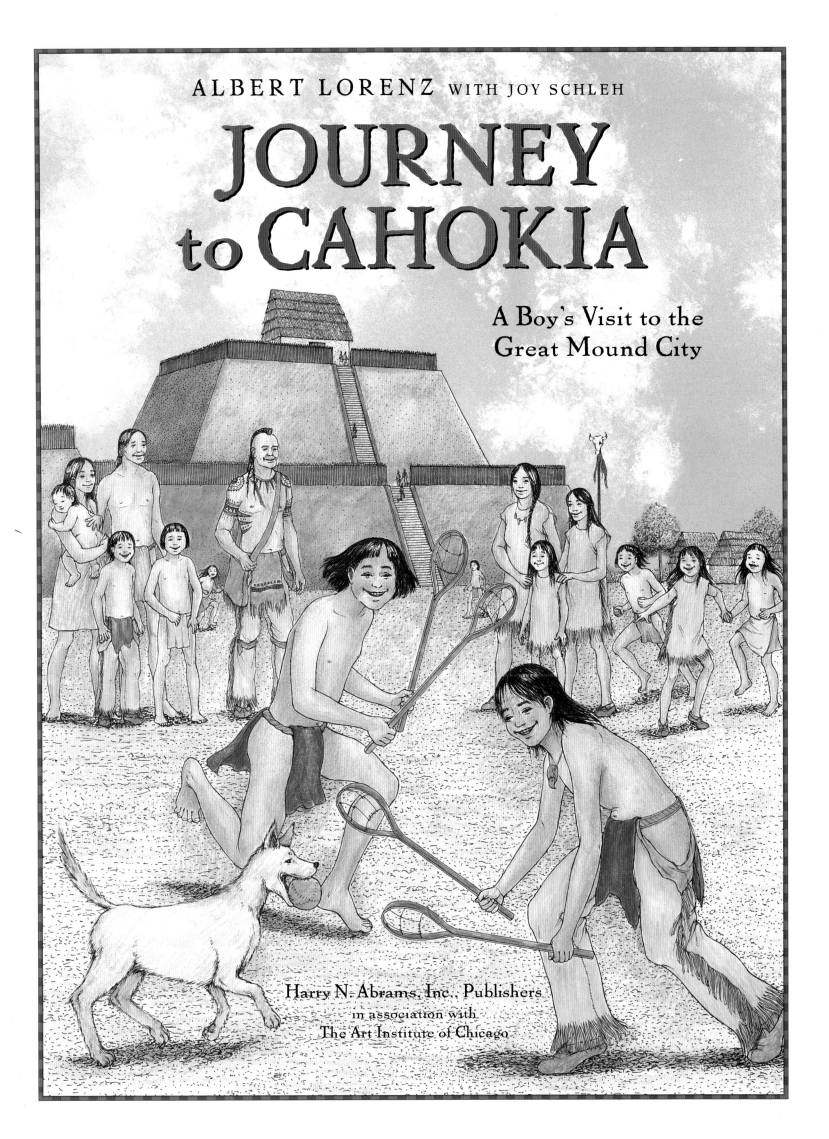

ALBERT LORENZ WITH JOY SCHLEH

JOURNEY to CAHOKIA

A Boy's Visit to the
Great Mound City

Harry N. Abrams, Inc., Publishers
in association with
The Art Institute of Chicago

LAKE MICHIGAN

In the two thousand years preceding the arrival of Europeans in North America, native Indian peoples created settlements across the broad expanse of the Midwest and Southeast. They included elaborate ceremonial grounds and numerous earthen mounds, and vast harnessed networks of trade stretching from the area that is today Minnesota and Wisconsin, south to the Gulf of Mexico, and from Oklahoma east to the Smoky Mountains of Tennessee and the Carolinas.

This book tells the story of one family's journey to the largest and most developed urban center, the ancient city of Cahokia along the Mississippi River, in approximately the year 1300 CE.

ILLINOIS

Illinois River

Missouri R.

Cahokia

MISSISSIPPI RIVER

Kaskaskia River

Wabash River

White River

Little Wabash R.

East Fork White River

Muscatatuck R.

THE RIVER WAS THE HIGHWAY FOR "MISSISSIPPIAN" PEOPLES AND CITIES C.1000-1600 CE.

Big Muddy River

Cavern in a Rock

Broad to the Falls

Rapids at the Falls

Beaver Po

OHIO

One Mile

Kentucky Lake

KEN

0   25   50
SCALE OF MILES

Mamma Cave

3000 BCE

SPHINX BUILT AT PYRAMID OF GIZA TO GUARD PHARAOH

c. 2500 BCE

STONEHENGE CONSTRUCTED IN SOUTHERN ENGLAND

c. 2100 BCE

ZIGGURAT AT UR (IRAQ)

c. 2000 BCE

HITTITES DEVELOP HORSE-DRAWN BATTLE CHARIOTS

c.1500 BCE

CLEOPATRA KILLS HERSELF WITH THE BITE OF AN ASP

30 BCE

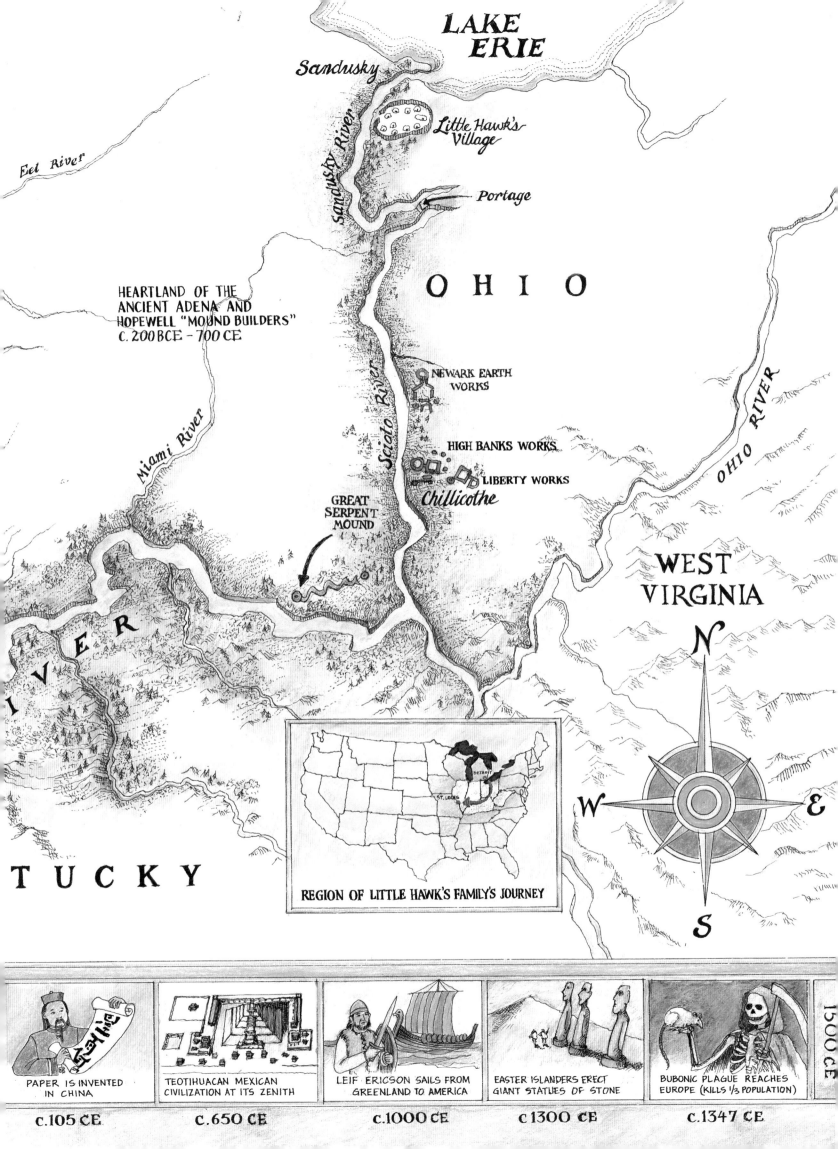

LAKE ERIE

Sandusky

Little Hawk's Village

Eel River

Sandusky River

Portage

O H I O

HEARTLAND OF THE ANCIENT ADENA AND HOPEWELL "MOUND BUILDERS" c. 200 BCE – 700 CE

NEWARK EARTH WORKS

Miami River

Scioto River

HIGH BANKS WORKS

LIBERTY WORKS

Chillicothe

GREAT SERPENT MOUND

OHIO RIVER

WEST VIRGINIA

IVER

N

W · E

S

TUCKY

DETROIT

ST. LOUIS

REGION OF LITTLE HAWK'S FAMILY'S JOURNEY

PAPER IS INVENTED IN CHINA

TEOTIHUACAN MEXICAN CIVILIZATION AT ITS ZENITH

LEIF ERICSON SAILS FROM GREENLAND TO AMERICA

EASTER ISLANDERS ERECT GIANT STATUES OF STONE

BUBONIC PLAGUE REACHES EUROPE (KILLS 1/3 POPULATION)

1500 CE

c. 105 CE   c. 650 CE   c. 1000 CE   c. 1300 CE   c. 1347 CE

Little Hawk stood in the middle of the village. There was still no sign of his father and the other men returning from the hunt. His father had promised that Little Hawk would join the hunters once winter came.

Little Hawk spotted his friend Small Otter and his father, White Feather, walking toward the river, carrying their spears and catching nets. They raised their open hands in greeting to Little Hawk, and he lifted his own hand in return.

As the sun climbed high overhead, Little Hawk watched his sister, Meadow Bird, and his mother, Spotted Fawn, make pots in which to store water, grains, and other items. Spotted Fawn wound long strands of clay into pots, then Meadow Bird would paint or engrave designs on them. Afterward, they would bake the pots in a hot fire to make them hard. Other girls and women performed similar tasks or pounded corn into meal or prepared animal skins to later cut into clothing.

Dogs began to bark. "Father!" cried Little Hawk. Sure enough, Red Earth, carrying several rabbits, walked into the clearing and joined his wife and children. Other men also were laden with squirrels and turkeys. The hunt had been successful.

After the evening meal, Gray Fox came to
Little Hawk's wigwam and said, "Red Earth,
we have been summoned to the council
house."

"May I come too?" pleaded Little Hawk.

"Yes," answered Red Earth. Joined by
White Feather, Small Otter, Gray Fox, and
Little Smoke, the men and boys walked
quickly toward the council house. Thick
smoke rose from the opening in the great
wigwam. This signaled the sacred fire of
Night Sky, the village shaman. Bear's Track,
the village chieftain, motioned the group
to enter.

"The harvest is over and our corn, meat,
fish, and grain are plentiful," said Bear's
Track. "You have brought the village many
beautiful furs of fox, beaver, martin, and
ermine. Night Sky read the sacred stones
and tells me the time is good for a trading
journey. I choose you to travel to the great
city of Cahokia and trade our furs and
copper for the goods we need. It will be a
long journey, two moons' time, so you will
take your families with you."

Little Hawk was thrilled. A trip to
Cahokia!

On the day of departure, Night Sky stood at the front of the crowd of villagers that gathered on the river's edge and waved a talisman over the canoes, asking for protection and success for the traders.

"Hurrah!" cried Little Hawk as the packed canoes slowly moved away from the bank. The journey to Cahokia had begun! The river's swift current carried the canoes, and Red Earth let Little Hawk and Meadow Bird take their turns at the paddles. The children watched in awe at the passing countryside— so different from their own.

Late one afternoon, Little Hawk saw something he had never seen before. In the distance above the shoreline, the earth had been molded into a number of shapes. One mound was rounded as if the moon had fallen to earth and been covered with dirt. The other shapes were ovals and rings—all formed of earth. The area was deserted and overgrown. He yelled to get the attention of the other families and pointed toward the mysterious mounds. The others stopped paddling to gape at the curious sight.

Little Hawk asked, "Father, what are those huge mounds? Who made them and why?"

"I don't know, son," he answered. "I've heard that there are great mounds formed with earth in the city of Cahokia. Perhaps we will find answers there."

That evening, as the families gathered around the open fire for warmth, the children begged Spotted Fawn for a story about their favorite hero, Red Horn.

"Long ago," began Spotted Fawn, "Chief Great Eagle said that he would hold a race to see who would marry his daughter. The winner would have to be the bravest and fastest hunter. Many braves entered the race, including a family of ten brothers. Kunu was the oldest and strongest. The youngest was slow and weak and called He-Who-Gets-Hit-With-Deer-Lungs. His brothers told him he need not enter the contest, but He-Who-Gets-Hit had a plan. On the day of the race, all the hunters ran and ran. They ran so far and so fast that they were running on the rim of the world. The youngest brother knew he could not run as fast as Kunu or the other hunters, but he had other strengths. He turned himself into an arrow and shot past all the hunters and won!

"Afterward, he stood before the whole village and announced, 'Those in the heavens named me He-Who-Wears-Human-Heads-as-Earrings.' With that he spat on his hands and as he began fingering his ears little faces appeared, laughing, winking, and sticking out their tongues. All the other braves were amazed. Then the youngest brother said, 'Those on Earth call me Red Horn.' With that he spat on his hands and drew them over his hair which became long and bright red. 'Kunu you are the oldest and, even though I won the race, you will marry Great Eagle's daughter.'

" 'Thank you, my little brother. From now on no one will call you He-Who-Gets-Hit-With-Deer-Lungs but you will always be called Red Horn.' All the brothers and all the villagers cheered for Red Horn. And that's how the hero got his name.

"Now, to sleep. We must be on our way again tomorrow," continued Spotted Fawn.

Several weeks passed as the villagers traveled down the river. It was now a wide expanse of water filled with traders from other villages going to or coming from the direction of Cahokia.

One morning, Little Hawk saw movement on the shore. "Father, look!" he cried. Several warriors began to wade into the river splashing the water with their spears and shouting loudly. They hoped the villagers would upset their canoes so they could rob them! Red Earth quickly guided the villagers' canoes close to the opposite shore. The attackers lacked canoes and their spears and arrows could not reach the villagers. Frustrated, they gave up the chase.

The villagers knew they were very near Cahokia.
Each child scanned the horizon, wanting to be the
first to see the great city. Late in the afternoon, as
they rounded a bend in the river, Meadow Bird
cried, "Cahokia!" Little Hawk and the others
gazed in amazement at a huge mound that rose
from behind a long stockade fence. Many people
lined the shore, packing and unpacking canoes.

Red Earth stood and held his open hand
toward the river's edge. Little Hawk knew this
signaled friendship. Several people on shore held
up their open hands toward the villagers and a
greeting party of two canoes, each manned by
some of Cahokia's warriors, paddled to meet them.

"If I truly were a hawk I could see the entire
city from the sky. I wonder what it would look
like," mused Little Hawk as he helped his father
guide the canoe to shore. The Cahokians helped
with the unloading of the canoes and took charge
of their guests. Two tall, magnificently tattooed
and feathered Cahokia warriors led the party to
the waiting officials of the city.

Little Hawk was amazed by everything he saw.
There were so many, many people, and they had
not yet entered the city's walls! Living in a village
of two hundred people had not prepared him or the
other villagers for the sight of this city of
perhaps twenty thousand.

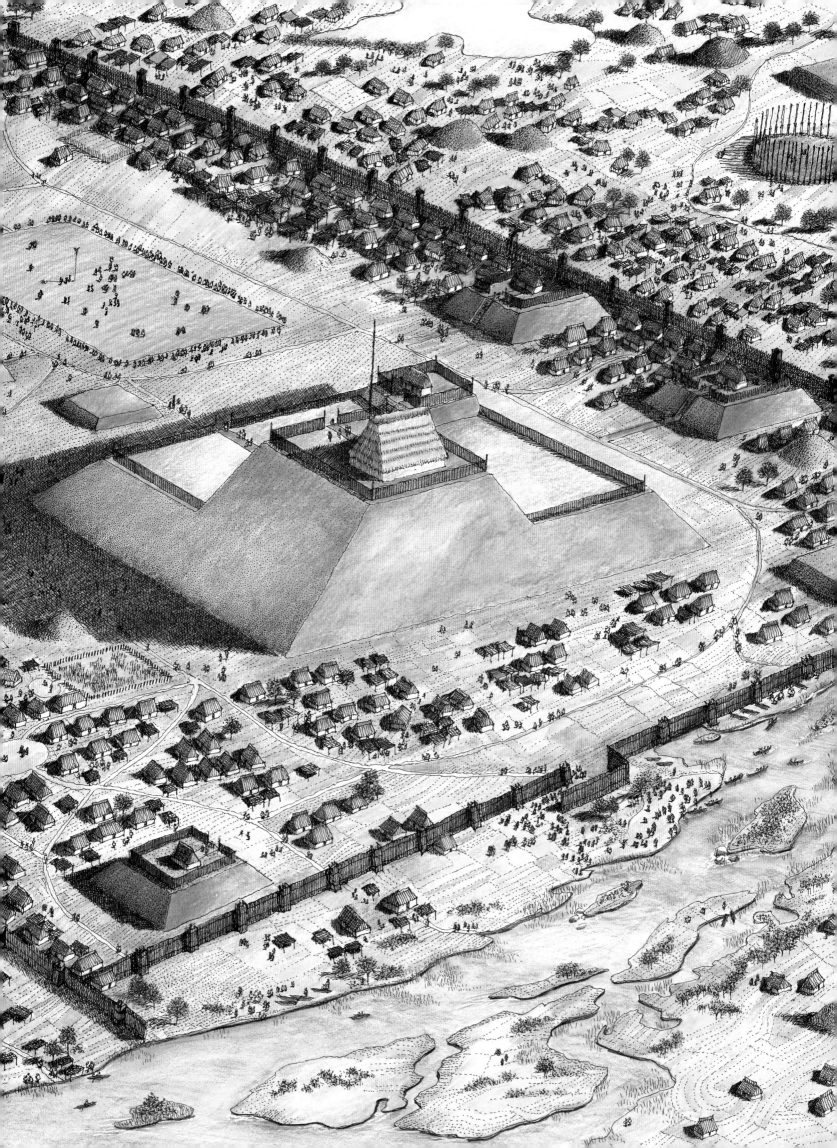

Upon entering the city, the villagers were taken to two spacious cottages. These were not wigwams like the villagers built, but buildings of tightly set wooden poles plastered with clay and roofed with thatched straw. All the men studied the structures, wondering if these buildings would be better protection from the cold winter than their own wigwams.

As they unpacked their belongings, two men came to greet them. One was a guide to welcome them, and the other a translator to make communication easier. The guide proudly explained that he would lead them on a tour of Cahokia and that they were to be honored guests at the coronation of Great Sun, Cahokia's new chief. This was indeed a privilege, and Little Hawk could see that his father was pleased and proud.

Their host led the villagers along a street toward a large open plaza. Along the way, Little Hawk and the others stopped to watch a group of young men and older boys, running, shouting, and laughing, engaged in some sort of organized game in an open field. All the players carried poles with nets on one end. They used these to toss a small leather ball toward other players who caught the ball in their nets, running all the while.

"What game is this?" asked Little Hawk.

"It is called lacrosse and all the boys in Cahokia love to play it," their host answered.

Little Hawk looked around with great curiosity as the group walked through the endless streets crowded with adults and children and lined with homes and platform-mounds of varying heights and sizes. Some of the buildings appeared to be quite large, but others were larger still and even more impressive. Little Hawk supposed these to be temples or medicine lodges. They passed homes of different sizes, each with a garden plot alongside, overflowing with corn, squash, beans, and pumpkins.

"These people are good farmers," Spotted Fawn remarked to Meadow Bird. She nudged her daughter as they passed a woman working the soil with an unusual-looking tool. Both of them noticed it again and again whenever they saw someone tilling soil in their garden.

"Look how quickly and easily the soil is tilled," Little Hawk overheard his mother tell Red Earth. "We must trade for this tool."

The villagers spent the next few days exploring the city and trading with the craftsmen in the plaza. They spread on the ground the copper and furs that they had brought for the city's residents to examine. The metal and fur pleased artisans who traded their conch shells, beautiful feathers, brilliant stones, beads, and carved pipes for them. Red Earth traded two of his fox pelts for three of the farming tools they had seen while walking the previous day. Holding one in his hand, he studied how the flint stone was shaped to a sharp edge and tied with hide to the wooden handle.

"This will make it easier to prepare the earth for planting. I will give two to Bear's Track when we return," he told his son. Little Hawk traded his arrows for a lacrosse pole and small ball. Spotted Fawn traded one of her baskets for a bottle sculpted in the shape of a mother nursing her baby. "Look, Meadow Bird, isn't this fine and beautiful? I will store our drinking water in it for our wigwam," she told her daughter.

Little Hawk saw a line of men carrying large baskets on their backs. "What are they doing?" he asked the guide.

"They are building a new burial mound," he responded. "The workers fill baskets with earth and carry it to the site."

Arrowheads such as these found at Cahokia were made of chert from quarries near St. Louis and from other beautifully colored hard stones that came from as far away as Arkansas and Oklahoma.

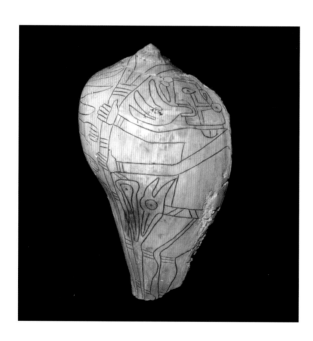

Ceremonial drinking cups, engraved with scenes of ritual performances, were often made from large conch shells gathered from coastal areas along the Gulf of Mexico.

Elaborate headdresses, such as this mask of a human face with deer antlers, and eyes and mouth inlaid with shell, were worn during ritual dances for the hunt or made to commemorate powerful and sacred ancestors, chieftains, or heroes who were themselves great hunters.

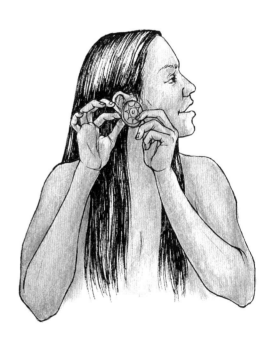

Earspools and earplugs, buttoned through the earlobe, were a common form of body decoration for ancient Native Americans, whether made of copper, wood covered in copper, mica, bone, or, as shown here, valuable stone.

The next day, the villagers joined the Cahokians as they congregated in front of the great pyramid. Little Hawk and his family and friends had never seen so many people in one place. The guide led the villagers to a spot that afforded an excellent view of the proceedings.

First, everyone turned to the south as the crowds parted to allow a tall regal warrior to pass. Great Sun! He quickly ascended to the top of the pyramid without pause. He turned and hailed his people, who cheered and chanted their approval. Never had the villagers experienced the noise such a large group could make. A priest placed a robe on Great Sun's shoulders. He addressed the multitude: "People of Cahokia, today is a glorious day for us. The Sun led our ancestors to this land long ago. We have honored her by building slanting hills of earth and sacred burial mounds, and she rewarded us with animals to hunt and rain for our crops and plentiful fish in our rivers. Great Sun is now our leader and he reveres the Sun's spirit. Great Sun says to celebrate this day in her honor."

Dancers, animal impersonators, and games took over the plaza and streets. The smells from cooking fires filled everyone with anticipation of the feast to come.

The next day the early morning was overcast and chill. Little Hawk and the other villagers knew that they must hurry home to avoid the coming winter snow. Everyone packed the canoes with the help of the guide and several of Cahokia's warriors.

Little Hawk and Meadow Bird were given a puppy and a cage of small birds as parting gifts from the Cahokian guide. Red Earth surprised Little Hawk with a hawk necklace.

"This is your spirit guide," Red Earth told him. "He helped you see the warriors on the river's bank and call the alarm, and he will help you in the future as you learn to hunt. Wear this necklace proudly."

Little Hawk beamed, honored by his father's gift. He was eager to return to his village and share with his friends what he had seen—and to wait for the first snows, when he, Little Hawk, would join the hunt.

Author's Note

When my editor contacted me about an exhibition that The Art Institute of Chicago was creating on the life and culture of the Native Americans known as "the mound builders," I was very excited. These mounds had long fascinated me. I was put in touch with Richard Townsend, the exhibition curator. He told me his plan for the show was to describe the Native American peoples and cultures of the great city of Cahokia; other early developments in the surrounding area, including the present states of Ohio, Tennessee, Georgia, Mississippi, Alabama, Louisiana, and Oklahoma; and the area that is today the Midwest and Greater Southwest. Of course, a book this size could not reflect a subject as vast as the exhibition. The show would be a journey of discovery for the visitors to the Art Institute, and I felt it should be the same for the young readers of the book as well. So, a family's journey presented itself as a workable vehicle for the storyline. I thought a young boy's eyes would serve as the best lens. The trip would be a trading mission and begin in what is now present-day Detroit and continue to Cahokia using the Native American highways of the time, rivers and streams.

The mythic Native American known as Red Horn is depicted here in this sculpture of flintclay that was discovered in eastern Oklahoma.

The great mound city of Cahokia, along the Mississippi River, thrived from 800 to 1400 CE in what is now Central United States. The city and its inhabitants had almost completely vanished by the time the first European explorations of the Americas began. What happened to the community is the subject of much speculation. Also debated is the function of many of the found artifacts as well as the purpose of the mounds themselves. Through the work of people such as Townsend, the lives of these people have slowly come to light. I felt strongly that the details of the mound builders needed to be distinctly illustrated in a historically accurate setting. I was provided a multitude of photographs of archival pieces to help me decide what types of things to place in the marketplace, what the people would wear, how the body tattoos would appear, and how the canoes, homes, and other buildings and defenses were constructed.

Archaeologists separate mound-builder communities into a hierarchy of four types. In ascending order, the least developed fourth line community was a small moundless site that consisted of a few structures surrounding a courtyard. The third line community, a village of several hundred people usually situated on a stream or lake, was made up of homes built around a small plaza often including one mound. The second line community was a regional center boasting a population of possibly thousands and had an impressive plaza with several mounds. The highly developed first

Ceramic vessels, such as this one in the form of a spotted deer, were made by Native Americans in Missouri, Arkansas, Tennessee, Mississippi, Alabama, and elsewhere in the shape of turtles, dogs, frogs, bears, owls, and fish.

line community was a great capital of politics, religion, commerce, and art with many neighborhoods, plazas, and permanent structures including mounds and temples. Cahokia is the only known first line community in North American history. At the height of the Cahokian culture, approximately 1000 CE, the population was over 20,000 people, making the city one of the great urban centers of the world at the time (larger than London!). Until 1800 CE no city in North America exceeded this size.

I had my small group of families travel from a fourth line community to the great first line community of Cahokia. This plan allowed all the wonder of Cahokia to be reflected in their reactions to the sights of this magnificent city. With the help of Townsend and the Art Institute's knowledgeable staff, I kept everything as accurate as possible, from the clothing, tattoos, and everyday life, even to the tales told around the fire.

I thank everyone who took time to provide me with information and critique my writing and illustrations. I wish to express gratitude to the following persons: Joy Schleh—my collaborator; Howard W. Reeves—my Abrams editor and friend; and the people at The Art Institute of Chicago: Richard F. Townsend, Curator of African and Amerindian Art, Leah Bowe (formerly of the AIC African and Amerindian Department), and Susan F. Rossen, Robert V. Sharp, and Amanda W. Freymann in the publications department. And especially to my wife, Maureen.

Jars, bowls, bottles, and other vessels were often elaborately decorated either through the stamping and engraving of designs into the surface of the clay or, as shown here, through boldly painted ceremonial signs or symbols such as sun circles, stars, crosses, hands, or skulls.

Bibliography

National Geographic:
>   "Mounds: Riddles from the Indian Past," by George E. Stuart, December 1972.
>   "America Before Columbus," by George E. Stuart, October 1991.

Cahokia City of the Sun, Cahokia Mounds Museum Society, Collinsville, Ill., 1999.

The Hero, the Hawk, the Open Hand: Mythic Art of Ancient North America, The Art Institute of Chicago, Planning Grant National Endowment for the Humanities, February 2001.

North American Indian Arts, by Andrew Hunter Whiteford, Golden Press, New York, N.Y., 1990.

Handbook of North American Indians, Smithsonian Institute, Volume 15 Northeast, Bruce G. Trigger, volume editor, Washington, D.C., 1978.

Native Tech: Scenes for the Eastern Woodlands, a Virtual Tour, by Tara Prindle, www.lib.uconn.edu/NativeTech/

Great Lakes Archaeology, by Ronald J. Mason, Department of Anthropology, Lawrence University, Academic Press, New York, N.Y., 1981.

American Indian Art Magazine:

"Tattooed Bodies & Severed Auricles: Images of Native American Body Modification in the Art of Benjamin West," by Arthur Einhorn and Thomas Abler, autumn 1998.

"Bonnets, Plumes, Headbands in West's Painting of Ferns Treaty," by Arthur Einhorn and Thomas Abler, summer 1996.

"Woven Mats of the Western Great Lakes," by Andrew Hunter Whiteford and Nora Rogers, autumn 1994.

"Woodland Artifacts 1738–1820," by J.C.H. King, winter 1991.

"Native Art as Depicted by Charles Hamilton Smith, 1816–1817," by J.C.H. King, spring 1994.

The George Catlin Book of American Indians, by Royal B. Hassrick, Watson-Guptill, New York, N.Y., 1977.

The Woodland Indians of the Western Great Lakes, by Robert Ritzenthaler, Pat Ritzenthaler, Milwaukee Public Museum, 1983.

Winnebago Hero Cycles: A Study in Aboriginal Literature, by Paul Radin, Indiana University Publications, Waverly Press, Baltimore, 1948.

The Native American Heritage: A Survey of North American Indian Art, by Evan M. Maurer, The Art Institute of Chicago, 1977.

Native North American Art History: Selected Readings, by Zena Pearlstone Mathews, New York University, and Aidona Jonaitis, State University of New York at Stony Brook, Peek Publications, Palo Alto, Calif., 1982.

Dedicated to the memory of Barney Plotkin

Photograph credits:
Page 24, top: Illinois State Museum Research and Collections Center, Springfield; photograph © 2003 by John Bigelow Taylor, New York; bottom: Smithsonian Institution, National Museum of the American Indian, Washington, D.C.; photograph © 2003 by John Bigelow Taylor, New York. Page 25, top: Smithsonian Institution, National Museum of the American Indian, Washington, D.C.; photograph © 2003 by John Bigelow Taylor, New York; bottom: Private Collection, Missouri; photograph © 2003 by John Bigelow Taylor, New York. Page 30, top: University of Arkansas Museum, photograph © 2002 by John Bigelow Taylor, New York; bottom: Westbrook Collection; photograph by David Dye, Memphis. Page 31: Private Collection, Missouri; photograph by David Dye, Memphis.

Designer: Ed Miller
Production Manager: Jonathan Lopes

Library of Congress Cataloging-in-Publication Data

Lorenz, Albert, 1941–
  Journey to Cahokia : a young boy's visit to the great mound city / Albert Lorenz ; with Joy Schleh.
    p. cm.
  Summary: In ca. 1300, Little Hawk and his family take a trip to trade with the Indians of Cahokia, the great city along the Mississippi River.
  ISBN 0-8109-5047-2
  1. Indians of North America—Mississippi River Valley—Juvenile fiction. [1. Indians of North America—Mississippi River Valley—Fiction. 2. Mississippian culture—Fiction.] I. Schleh, Joy. II. Title.

PZ7.L8828Jo 2004
[Fic]—dc22
                    2004005847

ISBN 0-8109-5047-2

Printed and bound in China
10 9 8 7 6 5 4 3 2

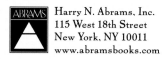

Harry N. Abrams, Inc.
115 West 18th Street
New York, NY 10011
www.abramsbooks.com

Abrams is a subsidiary of

LA MARTINIÈRE
GROUPE